Hold me Heal Me

By
Lindy Morelli

Copyright © 2024 Lindy Morelli
LCCN# 2024920448
All rights reserved.

No portion of this book may be reproduced in any form without written permission from the publisher or author except as permitted by U.S. copyright law.

WHAT IS THIS BOOK GOING TO BE ABOUT:

The purpose of this book is to comfort those who are going through intense pain of any kind, or prolonged chronic illness.

How will I do this?

I will write about the following topics.

1. Empathy for those lying sick in bed, day after day, year after year.

2. How to not lose hope when the treatment goes wrong and causes more problems.

3. How to make the time useful, and not give up when you feel you are doing nothing but suffering with your life.

4. How to deal with pain that seems and feels like it is endless.

5. What is the purpose of this pain.

6. How to redeem the time and use it wisely.

7. How to rejoice in the midst of this illness.

8. This illness; is it to die, or for the glory of God?

9. How to navigate this illness and heal fully if that is what I have discerned is my God-given purpose.

10. Or how to prepare to be held by God's everlasting ever-loving arms?

11. Purpose of this book: Who am I writing it for?

12. Those who are ill. It could be for cancer or any other terminally ill person, or it could be for someone who has a chronic illness or chronic pain; or it could be for anyone who has prolonged pain of any kind that doesn't go away, thought it would primarily be for someone struggling with illness, though I strongly object to that word and will write about why in the introduction.

13. I will write so that I can comfort people in these situations; people with pain that they live with every day, and people who are terminally ill and getting ready to meet God and be born into eternal life, so that I can offer them true comfort in God.

WHY AM I WRITING THIS?

I am writing it to comfort them and give them hope and skills and a way to thrive, despite illness.

What will I offer in this book?

Spiritual and emotional tools on how to get through and be happy.

And hope for heaven.

Amen.

TABLE OF CONTENTS

INTRODUCTION

Welcome to "Hold Me Heal Me".

Welcome to love, comfort, and hope in the midst of illness and pain.

If you are reading this book, you are ill or suffering and may ave been so for a long time.

You are searching for comfort, hope, and purpose in the midst of pain that feels endless.

Well, I have good news.

I have experienced a long-term illness, as well as severe emotional, physical, and spiritual pain, and I am thriving in the midst of it.

"What!" you may exclaim. "That can't be true! It isn't possible, and you must be crazy" (you shoot back.), that is, if you have the energy to even muster up a response. I know how hard it is, and I sure do know what it is like to feel so utterly exhausted and destroyed by illness that you can't even form a coherent thought.

Yet, even so, this book is about thriving and living, not dying, even if you are nearing the end of your life.

Here is my story in brief. I am sure you can relate to all of this, even if your illness and circumstances differ.

I have been blind since birth, so I know what living with a disability is. I know what it is like to be different from everyone else, to have to do things differently than others, and to have to often struggle through simple tasks. Yet, since I was fortunate enough to have received a wonderful education and training in life skills, living with total blindness is not really a big deal, even though it may present challenges.

The only reason I mention it here is so that you can get a full picture of my life circumstances, and the context in which I am writing.

I have found ways to adapt to life as a blind person, and this book really isn't about that.

Still, when illness comes, any little hindrance can make it worse.

If a person is sight-impaired or hearing-impaired, for example, and they become ill for any reason, of course, they will experience the illness with the added challenge of being hindered by a disability.

If they cannot see, they cannot easily get to doctors and may have to spend a lot of energy or money working out transportation.

If they cannot hear, they may have a hard time communicating with their doctor and may often be misunderstood; the list can go on and on, but this is only something I just want to make note of as something that can compound the difficulty of a chronic or terminal illness.

By the way, I am not really sold on the word "chronic." I don't like it, in fact, and the reason is that it sounds so hopeless and dark.

When someone first mentioned to me that I had a "chronic" illness, I was shocked and greatly distressed.

"Chronic" just sounds like there will never be any way out; no improvement, and how can a person possibly deal with that?

It is something like death or dying every day, except that it is for the rest of your life because it is so-called "chronic", and what are you supposed to do about all that anyway?

Well, sometimes illnesses and symptoms don't really ever go fully away, but they can be managed.

Should they be called "chronic?" I don't really know.

All I know is that I have had to learn to live with persistent debilitating symptoms of illness, which I have had for several years, and there doesn't seem to be any cure as of yet.

So, whatever you want to call it, the trick is to have hope and to still live when you are feeling awful every day and not let this awful ill feeling beat you down or ruin your life.

How can a person do that, you may ask? Well, I will tell you in these pages how I am doing it.

It seems that my story of "illness" started when I was young, but it didn't seem to take over till my mid-fifties. In 2016, I was diagnosed with secondary adrenal insufficiency. (Incidentally, this type of adrenal problem is different than Addison's disease. Some people call it adrenal fatigue, but technically, adrenal insufficiency is different from adrenal fatigue.) But that isn't important here. What is important is that this diagnosis, along with one called "central nervous system sensitization syndrome," caused me to become severely limited and seriously debilitated. Also, in 2022, I got COVID-19, which turned into long-term COVID-19. Then, a few months later, I was diagnosed with chronic Lyme Disease. At the time of this writing, I am searching and working with doctors to see if I have dysautonomia and small tissue fibro disease, but regardless of whatever diagnoses I may receive, in a certain sense, all these labels don't really matter. They may provide a way of perhaps making sense of the symptoms I experience, but in the end, it is about managing these symptoms and not being overcome by them.

Anyway, earlier in my life, in my twenties, I had had mono, like so many others, and at the time, I couldn't get my strength back. The doctors said I had Epstein-Barr, but they couldn't do anything about it.

Throughout my life, I had had periods when I felt completely exhausted, and as my thirties and forties progressed, I felt weaker, but I only realized in hindsight that I had felt that way, off and on, for years. I was working very hard and didn't really expect illness to creep up on me. From 2016, when I got the first diagnosis, I just kept getting sicker and sicker. Little things were getting harder and harder, and no matter what kind of doctors I went to or what kind of natural treatments I received, things just kept getting worse until my health came crashing down in 2020, right before the COVID pandemic erupted globally.

I couldn't go out, be in crowds, or tolerate conversation, stimulation, smells, sounds, or noise of any kind. I could not read or listen to music to help pass the time. I simply could not handle any stress, and depending on how stressful any given day is, even now, as I write this book, I may be pushed back into the same physical state, even if the source of that stress is from good things. Suppose events are too stressful, or there is too much activity on a certain day, or a period of a couple of days in a row. In that case, I have to lie in bed a large part of the following day to get my strength back, and it could take up to two weeks, or a month, to recover from too many days of too much activity or stress. When I was at my worst, and before I knew how to manage the symptoms, I had to be in complete silence most of the time because too much conversation about anything, even about the smallest thing, like what I wanted to eat or where I want someone to put my mail when they had picked it up for me, was too much.

Getting the energy to do the smallest thing, like dragging myself up to get a drink of water or to eat a piece of fruit, was astronomically difficult and often still is.

Just hearing about anything painful in the world, such as an accident at a factory, for example, among people I didn't even know personally, can cause me excruciating pain. I guess you could say that I qualify as a highly sensitive person, for sure.

I can often feel my heart race as soon as anyone brings up anything the least bit painful, such as talking about someone with the Coronavirus or about someone who is having marriage problems. Even if these things are just alluded to in the briefest way, it can make me feel extremely ill immediately.

As I write this, however, even though my health is fragile and I am very sensitive, as I have said, I am very happy.

How could that be? You may ask and be skeptical. "What is helping you through this illness?" you may ask. "Where does real healing come from anyway?"

Well, read on, my friend, and you will find out.

Lindy Morelli

DEDICATION

O Blessed Virgin Mary, my Mother, most Tender-hearted, I dedicate this book to you with every beat of my heart, with every drop of my blood.

May you use it as you see fit. Amen. You are my hope.

CHAPTER ONE

CHILLED TO THE BONE AND THE SOUL

Hope For The Journey From One Who Knows

What are you going through, my friend, my dear friend? Yes, since we are all truly connected as brothers and sisters in Christ, it really is that way; we are friends. Whatever you are going through is part and parcel to me. I feel it in my bones and in my soul.

Do you have cancer, depression, or AIDS? Do you have a disability that keeps you from walking or going outside into the sunshine?

Oh! How I understand! I really, truly do. I never thought I'd be this way, weakened and feeling so ill every day. All my life, I was athletic. I was vibrant and active, and I did all kinds of things. I liked to hike, swim, do many arts and crafts, write poetry, play in musical groups at church, make meals for needy people, etc.

But in my middle fifties, I came down with this illness.

It stopped me in my tracks, and I couldn't do everything I loved anymore.

All I could think about was how sick I felt every day and every night.

The doctor said: "You will have some bad times. It isn't terminal, but you are like a person who needs to be in a long-term retreat, where you can get good rest, good food, and have no stress."

"What type of place is that?" I remember asking in a daze.

"Well, in the old days, they used to have sanitariums, where people could just go to recuperate, but they don't have them anymore," the doctors explained. So, I had to make my home into a makeshift respite/retreat, which I've been doing for quite a while.

I am rarely out in crowds. I am content with the way things are. At first, it was hard, though, since I wasn't used to everything hurting so much.

In the beginning, I was miserable at every moment of the day. Nothing brought me comfort except quiet. I couldn't eat, and the smell of food made me sick, and often still does. I lived on protein drinks, chicken broth, apple juice, and cooked vegetables for over two years.

When this all started, life was very sad and difficult. I wondered if I would ever feel better. So, yes, I understand what it is like to suffer on all levels because this illness came about, in some respects, at least, as a result of extreme tragedy and stress. So as not to get side-tracked, I'll spare you the details. I guess you'll have to read one of my other books to find out about all that if you're interested. But anyway, the thing is that stress can really do a person in.

I didn't know if I would ever get better, and my life was ebbing away. I couldn't talk to friends, and even going out to the doctor or the bank was a major hardship.

I feel the pain of everyone who is ill and suffering in any way, of everyone who is lying in bed all alone.

So, how did I get in a good enough place to even start writing this book, you may ask? Well, to be honest, I started writing in desperation, believing that this illness had a purpose. We all have challenges. We are all put here for a reason, so I wasn't going to just give up and quit.

What do you think, my friend? Do you really want to just give up and quit? How boring and empty life would be if you decided to do that every day, just lying in bed, hurting, and thinking of nothing except your own pain and misery?

What do you think of that option? It sounds pretty dismal, doesn't it? Believe it or not, there are other really good options.

CHAPTER TWO

BUMPS IN THE ROAD

How to overcome the ups and downs.

So, it seems that I can safely conclude that if you continue to read this book, you are, at least in some respects, open to searching for other better options.

And that being the case: "What next?" you may ask, trying to rally and summon your strength. Well, my friend, if you have made the decision, at least for today, to try to think of something other than your pain, just getting out of bed or getting something to eat may be a major accomplishment. I surely understand. I truly do.

But whatever you can do today, try to do it.

Of course, there are bumps in the road as you go along, and when you are in pain, you feel every little bump like a mountain. Just going really slowly and gently with yourself, no matter what you are doing or how you think, will help you a lot. Things can be overwhelming when you have an illness, so just be as patient and kind to yourself as you can.

I discovered that there are things that happen along the way in illness and pain that no one can be prepared for. How about when doctors prescribe treatments that make you sicker and do no good? I certainly went through that, maybe not to the magnitude you did; but still, suffering is suffering, and no one can compare crosses, I don't think.

Doctors mean well but are limited and can only do so much. At one point, I was on 23 supplements (or you may be on 23 different medications if that is the type of medical intervention you are undergoing), and the treatment was making me worse and worse.

It is terrible and crazy when something that you trust to help you doesn't work. Everything starts going wrong; everything. My hair fell out a few years ago. Being unable to eat and feeling too sick to walk across the room is hard.

How do you hang in there when things get worse? You just keep putting one foot in front of the other. One thing I can say is that you must trust yourself.

I know that we all deal with health care differently. I have chosen to work with Integrative functional medical doctors; that is, doctors who respect my right to trust my own knowledge and intuition about the illnesses I have been diagnosed with. I work with doctors who respect my ability to research my health challenges and my need for what will help me.

There is plenty of information about even rare health conditions online, and there are always various treatment options. Integrative doctors work with both conventional medicine and alternative forms of care. I believe both approaches are needed to get the best results, and being proactive about one's treatment and healing is paramount.

We are not machines. One size doesn't fit all, in my opinion. We are people with minds and hearts. We must listen to our intuition and bodies to know what is best.

So, if you are encountering a prescribed treatment that isn't working, my best advice is to pray for guidance and do your own digging to find what will best help you.

Don't take the doctor's word for it without trying to help your-self.

Above all, don't give up.

If you give up, the pain will beat you, and you will have no hope of recovery.

My friend, don't you think it's pretty good news that you can actually do something to help yourself, even if you thought you could not? Really! Your healing is more under your control than you think it is.

Every day, start looking for the good.

Start looking for the smallest thing that is helping you, such as, "I sat out in the sun today. I was able to eat a piece of bread for the first time in two months. I was able to move my arm today. I smiled today," etc.

Look at those things and thank God and always remember how far looking at such things goes, because keeping your focus on the good will boost up your hope.

By the way, I really care.

I really do.

I really comprehend how pain can be.

So, what do you do when everything's going wrong? There are just too many mountains to climb in one day!

Well, as I said, we can't compare crosses. I wasn't diagnosed with cancer, and I didn't go through chemo. I don't know what it is like to go through chemo year after year, be sick for months, and have all kinds of side effects from chemo. I wasn't diagnosed with chronic depression, and I don't have personal experience of trying to pull myself out of that "black hole." But I do know what it is like to be very ill with extreme pain most days, for months and years on end.

We all must make our own decisions about what will help us heal.

Sometimes, the treatment is worse than the illness itself. But if you really believe in that treatment and believe it will help you, you've got to keep believing with all your heart. Don't give up. You must keep fighting.

Still, for me, though, compared to ongoing painful, horrifically difficult treatments, I only had a comparatively limited taste of what it is like to follow treatment for the illnesses I experience and then make things worse. In any case, whether you have several years of nothing working or just a few months of extreme pain and frustration and/or repeated episodes of those few months, it isn't fun.

What do you do when you are sick from whatever medication was prescribed, and you are getting sicker, not better? You could feel like giving up when nothing is helping.

"Will this illness or pain ever go away?" you may ask in exasperation. You can feel angry and disgusted and just wonder why bother. "I will probably always be ill."

But such thoughts won't help. You can't push negative thoughts away, but just the same, they will most certainly kill you if you don't find a way to deal with them.

You have to realize that negativity is part of the killer. You just must recognize negativity for what it is and say to yourself, "There it is again, that negativity, but I don't want to choose that line of thinking, and I am going to change it into something positive and into gratitude."

Find something to be grateful for, even if it's drinking some soup you like the taste of, or maybe someone did something kind for you today, like stopping over to say hi or smiling at you when you went out to give blood.

Just put your mind on gratitude and use your common sense when the treatment goes wrong.

Don't be afraid to follow your judgment. Doctors do a wonderful job, but they aren't in your body or experiencing what you are experiencing.

Be proactive about your illness and your healing. Do some research about your condition, and find out what will help you. Don't expect to be passive and let the doctors do all the work. Don't just lie there and let yourself do nothing. You won't overcome the bumps in the road that way.

Remember, you are a whole person, even if you are in pain, ill, or have a disability.

You have a mind, and you can still think if you are reading this book.

You have a heart, and you have a will.

Use your mind and will in a positive way. Ask yourself what will really help you. Find the things that work for you and eliminate the things that don't.

Make your own decisions and take ownership of your well-being, no matter how small the steps you feel you can take.

Perhaps all you can do today is push the remote button to change the channel from the awful news station, or to the rotten movie on television.

Well, at least, for Heaven's sake, do that! And put something nice on to watch to make you feel good inside.

Ask yourself: what can I do right now? What will make me feel even the tiniest bit better? Is it to drink some water or sing a little song of faith to yourself? Is it to glance at some pictures in a magazine or call a friend? Well, whatever it is, just think of whatever you can do or give, no matter how small it may be.

Is it to thank the nurse who helps you dress or fold your blanket when you get up so that it isn't a mess when you go back to bed? Believe it or not, even something like that will help because you will feel more in control and less disorganized and cluttered in your surroundings.

Just think and use your imagination.

You can do it.

I know you can.

I am rooting for you all the while.

CHAPTER THREE

WHEN THE PAIN SEEMS ENDLESS

What to do when all you feel you are doing is suffering with your life.

Yes, I'm sure you know how it feels when it feels like all you are doing is suffering. We have all been there, haven't we? There is no doubt about it.

As soon as I wake up, I may feel pain in my body and sickness in my soul, just sickness, weakness, pain, terrible pain in my muscles, joints, bones, organs, and nerves. Pain in my psyche and spirit, because what awaits me? Just endless suffering?

It is hard to describe illness, and because everyone suffers differently and experiences pain differently, it is hard to write about what you are going through because I am not you. I just know for myself that pain is pain. I am conscious of it as soon as my eyes blink open or if I lie awake all night; because of it, I am conscious of it, and there is no escape.

How do I keep from going crazy with this pain?

Pain that gnaws at my insides like a raging inferno?

Once, I read that Saint Therese of Lisieux, one of my favorite people, said that the pain she suffered was so great; she could certainly see why people would be tempted to take their lives because how else could they escape it?

I am certainly not advocating that. I am just saying how weak we all are as human beings in the face of pain.

But my friend, there is only one way to get past all this: to look unceasingly at the Cross. If you can, hold a crucifix or a rosary in your hand. Cling to Jesus.

Cling to Him for all you are worth, and think constantly about every bloody part of His body and every deadly tortured part of His agonizing soul.

Look at Him! Look at Jesus! Talk to Him and tell Him that every pain, solitary tear you shed, and every frustrating moment of your life is for Him.

That is how the pain you and I are suffering now will turn into little golden drops of precious redeeming light and joy that will lift others from Hell and make Paradise a little closer with each breath and laborious step we now take.

But you may ask, how do I go on when the pain is endless; when the days, weeks, and months just seem like years?

Well, here's what I've discovered as an answer to that:

You know, when we are in pain, time hangs awfully heavy. The hands on the clock never seem to move. The days and nights just drag, and all we feel is pain.

But time is holding us captive, and we are trapped in it.

So, we must acquire a brand new outlook and obtain an eternal perspective. We must recognize that there is no such thing as time in God's economy. We must step out of the constructs and restrictions of seeing things through the question of "How long will this last?" and then step into the wide-open space of infinity and eternity.

In eternity, there is no time.

There is no measure of time, and there are no confines of space.

We are not trapped, and nothing is limited by time.

You may be thinking: "Well, then, if eternity is forever, with no constraints of space or time, then this pain, for sure, is endless, if eternity is endless." But that is not what I mean. What I mean is that since eternity is endless, it is also infinite. It is wide open to fathomless possibilities and boundless freedom. Eternity is the realm of never-ending joy and unforeseen miracles. What if your pain and mine are used for some great, eternal purpose? Something far beyond our comprehension? What if all that you are suffering now is like dynamite that heaven can use?

CHAPTER FOUR

GIVE ME LIGHT; I NEED IT

What Is the Purpose of This Pain?

"Well, if there is some unforeseen eternal purpose to this crushing, never-ending pain, what is its mysterious hidden purpose?" you may ask in frustration.

I have thought about this question for a long time myself.

I have heard really good people say that if all they are going to do is suffer in life, they might as well not live because what is the purpose of an empty life of pain and confinement to bed, or to some limitation which one cannot change?

But, so, what is the purpose anyway?

Surely, you have and are asking this question along with me.

Well, the purpose is this.

It is a wonderful, sublime purpose!

Are you ready to do something great with your life? No, I am not just trying to psych you up or give you a mental pep talk to make you feel better. I am writing to you about the truth, and the truth will set you and me free.

The purpose of this pain is so that we can all actually break chains and set ourselves and others free.

It is setting people free from everlasting suffering, sin, and death.

"What is sin?" you may ask. "Isn't that some religious anti-quated concept that someone just used to preach about long ago to make us all feel guilty? I don't believe in sin," you may say.

But let me ask you this:

What makes everyone so miserable?

What makes us all turn away from hope? What makes things go wrong in our lives and relationships? What brings misery to life, to big things, like when divorce comes into a family and marriages go wrong, leaving children shattered and the ones abandoned so sad? What makes everyday life so tedious and empty? Isn't it the little irritations that come to us every day, like when someone we work with is careless or selfish, and lots of little annoyances pile up until our heart is filled with weariness and resentment? Then everything just explodes and falls apart.

It is a sin that causes this, isn't it?

Surely, we are all missing the mark of the divine and true purpose for which we were originally made in not being able to truly love. We all suffer from a colossal, universal, fundamental wound that has left us broken. Just look around. Who is not touched and hurting from this wound? Do you know anyone? You may think someone next to you has everything perfect in their life, but that isn't true. Sometimes, we all fail and make mistakes that we can regret for a long time. Do you know anyone who hasn't made a mistake? Do you know anyone who is perfect?

Likewise, have you ever been caught in a habit that is hurting yourself or others, and no matter how hard you try to overcome it, you can't break free? The habit could be as simple as getting angry too quickly, having a short fuse, blowing up, and saying things you regret. It could be something like drinking too much or spending too much money. Whatever it is, we sometimes all find ourselves in patterns of behavior that bring us and others down, don't we?

Also, besides the fact that we all make mistakes and hurt each other, whether we want to admit it or not when we find ourselves inevitably on the receiving end of not having received enough love in our hearts or of not feeling loved, we are left empty, lonely and bereft, are we not? Not being loved by the people we need love from comes from the brokenness and shortcomings we all have as human beings, such as not being able to love each other as was originally intended. We were all meant to live in peace and harmony on earth, but it isn't that way down here. So, whatever you want to call the fundamental brokenness, woundedness, and inherent propensity, we all have to fall short of being able to love; it is there; it can't be avoided.

I think one could aptly define sin in practical terms as the absence of desperately needed Divine love.

So, wouldn't you want to free yourself and everyone else you can from this loneliness, emptiness, and tyranny of such a tragic dearth of divine love? Wouldn't you want to be part of the healing solution for the plight we all find ourselves in?

This is what you can actually do now with the bitterness and pain you are in: You can look at Jesus the Lord, hanging on the Cross for all time and through all eternity, and unite your pain, tears, agony, and suffering to His. You can offer your life, one moment at a time, all your sorrows to Him, yourself, and others who need your loving prayer.

This Divine love, that comes from Heaven above, is the only thing that can heal us all as human beings.

You can become part of the greatest power on earth, the power of giving and sharing true divine love. In every moment, by being strongly committed to moving your will toward loving your neighbor in the midst of this pain, you are one step away from finding your life's true purpose. It is tangible and at your fingertips, for in simply choosing to love where you are, in the condition and situation you find yourself in right now, you can truly give hope and freedom to people who need it. You can spread peace and goodness just by choosing to give and love. Wouldn't it be wonderful to live in a world where there is plenty of love and kindness to go around? So why not try to give and do what you can with what you have?

This may sound archaic, but it is the most powerful thing you can do. Believe it or not, it will actually make you happy and fill your heart with joy.

You will realize that your life has real meaning, a greater purpose than anything you could have done if you hadn't been afflicted with this pain and sickness. You will discover a true purpose far greater than if you had been living your life free to do whatever you want your own way.

After all, if you had not been afflicted with this pain or illness, you would still be calling the shots, wouldn't you? You wouldn't feel weak, incompetent, or useless; you would think you have it all together and that your life will last forever, but it will not.

You would still be full of your own ideas, as I have been all my life. I have been full of myself, basically. I desperately wanted to please God but was full of my own agendas and plans. When hardships came, I protested and didn't understand what God was doing. I found it almost impossible to accept my life as it was.

But now, in the midst of this suffering and pain, grace has opened my heart and given me light. I now know what my real purpose is; it is to live to free others. By lovingly offering to God whatever pain and sorrows I have, I can truly help others. Prayer like this is powerful. It spans all space and time. It reaches all people, no matter where they are, regardless of what condition they are in. As I give Jesus my entire will and unite my pain to His, I do this for all people, in all places and in all times. By having the genuine intention of being with Jesus in everything and by repeating the simple act of uniting all my suffering to His for all people, I have found the true purpose of my life. It is to help all people to be lifted up from the sad condition of living in this lonely world of misery and sin. It is to pray in the midst of this pain so that all may find love and be freed from the hopelessness of "NO Love." In this way, I can help to spread the lasting peace we have all been searching for.

Why don't you join me in this sublime purpose? You can live a life of hope and give that hope to others, taking one purpose-filled step at a time.

CHAPTER FIVE

TEMPUS FUGIT

How To Make The Time Count

What can you do when you spend your days in pain? How can you use the time purposefully and not die of boredom or hopelessness? Can you do anything of significance or substance at all, or is your life just a colossal waste of time?

I'm sure we have all grappled with these questions at one point or another. Here are some of the answers I've come up with.

Well, can you still move your hands or feet, or can you move any of your muscles?

If you cannot, do you still have your mind? Can you think clearly, at least some of the time?

What about your heart? Yes, it is still beating, isn't it?

With your heart, you can love. With your mind, you can love and read, and if you can move any of your muscles, you may be able to do some simple things. Perhaps you can make a pretty scarf out of yarn or whittle a well-crafted sandpiper out of soft wood. Maybe you can draw a picture or make someone a cheerful greeting card. You can create something special just from your ingenuity and unique ideas.

You can think of the people around you who you can help.

Maybe you can't work anymore outside your home at the job you used to have, but maybe you can help fold clothes for a single mother down the street. Maybe you can help your neighbor paint his old front porch on sunny days when you feel up to lending a hand. Even just an hour or two can be a big help and make you feel better.

I know that on most days, doing anything that requires any energy or thought, or just thinking about it, can feel impossible, and even the suggestion of something like what I mentioned above can be overwhelming just thinking about it. So, if you are too weak to do any of those things, don't worry. Just think of what you can do and do it with love.

Maybe all you can do is lie in bed all day and watch television. Perhaps all you can do is to be cheerful when someone comes in to help you with a daily chore. Believe it or not, watching TV with love and purpose can help others. If you are watching a movie or program you like, enjoy it the best you can. If you are in too much pain, just keep looking at the crucifix on your wall, or hold a crucifix in your hand, and tell Jesus, over and over, that you love Him and want to help Him save souls. This is the most important thing anyone can do, and you are doing the most crucial thing right where you are. It may be hidden from everyone else's physical eyes, but God sees all, and offering your suffering up in this way to God with acceptance and love is the most powerful thing you can do.

Think of what you can give every day, even if you feel it is small, and take pride in that. If all you can do is to smile and say "thank you" to someone who comes in to help you get dressed or clean your apartment, then say thank you and smile because, believe it or not, that is a much bigger thing than you think.

It isn't so much what we do or how much we do each day, but what matters most is the way we do what we do.

If all you can do is lie in bed most of the day, then pray for others who need your prayers. Think of things to say "thank you" to God for, and thank Him on behalf of all those in the world who are going through life blindly and not thanking Him for anything at all.

Remember that everything you do—taking your medicine, receiving treatments for your health, feeling pain in your body and soul, reading a book, getting dressed, going outside, watching a television program, listening to a friend, or anything at all—is sacred, holy, and blessed.

After all, in the end, we will not be asked what we did with our days and lives, but how we loved, and at every moment, in everything we do, we have a chance to do every little thing with love, even if it is just taking one breath in, and one breath out, one step forward, one small action at a time.

So, remember these things when the days feel long: Doing everything with love, every little thing, is the most meaningful way to make our time count.

CHAPTER SIX

HOW TO REJOICE IN THE MIDST OF THIS PAIN

"The joy of the Lord is my strength." (Nehemiah 8:10)

"Joy! What's that?" you may ask skeptically. "How can anyone have joy when they are in pain?" you may wonder incredulously.

Well, believe it or not, despite everything I've been through, I really do have joy, and I'm not just saying that to make you and me feel good.

You may be asking what joy actually is. Here is the answer, and this is the truth.

Joy is a supernatural gift that comes from God alone. It is a fruit of the Holy Spirit and doesn't leave, even when things go wrong.

It is a deep, abiding sense of knowing that we belong to God and that we live for God alone.

It is there even in the midst of suffering and sorrow, because its source is in the eternal God of love, who promises and delivers on His promise: His promise of everlasting life.

Our joy is based on a solid hope, just as it says in Saint Paul the Apostle's letter to the Romans (Romans 5). In these Scripture verses, we read about how suffering leads to patience, and patience leads to character development, and character development leads to hope; and about how true hope, which comes deep in the soul, through God's working in us, this true hope does not leave us disappointed, because it is rooted in the hope in eternal life. As we gain and have an eternal outlook on everything, including our pain, we are filled with joy, which is everlasting.

With this solid hope in the promise of eternal life and an eternal perspective, we need not despair. This joy never fades away, even when misfortunes come. It doesn't get weary and run out of steam when the going gets tough. It is joy that comes from God, and it is our strength!

If you need this type of joy, ask God to give it to you.

Pray sincerely, and you will receive it.

In my estimation, joy and gratitude go together. When you have joy and gratitude, you are strong. When you and I recognize and focus on the good things in our lives, we have joy and can overcome all darkness and pain.

You may think, "Well, there isn't anything to be grateful for. Why bother?"

Yes, I know.

Many people are depressed and don't see any purpose in life. They may be old or sick, and life is too hard and empty. They just don't see anything good or any reason to rejoice, but what I am saying is that true joy doesn't depend on circumstances or on whether things are going my way or not.

I could be in extreme suffering and pain but still have joy.

This is a spiritual gift.

Turn your eyes to Jesus and open your heart.

Pray and be open.

Remember how joyful and full of spontaneity little children are. They play in everything. They like to jump in puddles. They play when eating their cereal in the morning. They play when taking a bath, and they play when going for a walk. They like to skip and hop and jump like little bunnies, don't they?

They don't just walk sedately with long faces, like most adults, who are so serious and down in the dumps.

They play and have fun in everything. We can play and have fun too. Why not be like them and enjoy everything?

Though pain is present, it does not have to cancel out joy or dominate one's life. Jesus is the one true God, the one and only Lord, and the only one who should rule over our entire lives. If we have constant pain, then that pain should be absorbed into our love for Jesus and His love for us. Let this happen to you, and you will discover true joy.

You might say to yourself: "Well, how do I have fun when my body is in excruciating pain, and that is all I can think about?" Yes, well, for sure, I understand. Just remember what I said in the other chapters of this book. There is a purpose for this pain, and that purpose is eternity and Jesus. Once you give your heart to Jesus and give your life completely over to Him, you will see that your life has a great purpose and will want to participate fully in God's plan for you. Your heart will fill with gratitude, and you will find it much easier to be open to the gift of God's true joy.

Joy is in the heart, and it is abiding, even while there is pain.

If you don't believe me, give it a try.

Be small, like a child. Make yourself small. Forget about yourself and your own way of thinking. Tell Jesus you want Him to be Lord of everything—of your pain, thoughts, and whole life. Be like a little child and rejoice!

Ask for joy from God, and you will receive it.

A Christian should be always swimming in joy, according to a thought taken from Saint John of the Cross's writings. (He was one of the greatest Christian mystics from the 15th Century.)

"What! Are you crazy?" you may ask in astonishment. "How can a person feel any joy at all, let alone swim in it, when they are suffering the way I am?"

What did Saint John of the Cross mean when he said that anyway?

Well, I believe that what he meant is that heavenly joy is just that: from Heaven.

Joy comes from the Holy Spirit. It is a great gift from our loving God. It is not something you can conjure up yourself, and it is not something you can just talk yourself into. It is not of human origin. It is from God.

If you need this joy in the midst of your pain, ask God for it, and He will give it to you.

In Matthew 7:7 we read that God never denies the Holy Spirit to anyone who asks Him for it, and that whole story is about God being a good and loving father who, when His son asks for an egg, would not give him a stone; or when his friend asks for a loaf of bread at night, though his friend might eventually get up and give him something to eat, just because he is annoyed by his friend's constant knocking, God, who is not just listening to our prayers out of a sense of obligation, but out of love, will surely give us whatever we need, especially in times of desperation, when we persevere in asking.

So, ask for joy if you don't have any.

Joy is a great grace!

It is not dependent on external circumstances. The ups and downs of life are changeable from hour to hour, and our feelings change from moment to moment, day to day.

But when we have the peace and joy of the Holy Spirit in our hearts, when we are solidly rooted in Jesus, we have joy.

This joy is true, real, and lasting.

It doesn't fade away in the midst of sorrow or suffering, and no amount of physical, emotional, or spiritual pain can blot it out.

In Nehemiah, we read that the joy of the Lord is our strength. We also remember that Mother Theresa of Calcutta said that there is so much to give others in just our simple smile.

Why is a smile so beautiful, and why is laughter so important.? I am sure you have heard it said that laughter is the best medicine or that laughter is the medicine for the soul.

Smiling can brighten up a room, and if you just smile, even half-way, it has been scientifically proven that It helps your mood. It is like telling your brain that it is okay to be at ease and relax.

Smiling and laughing is good for us all, and when we come to know that everything in our life has eternal value, well, that simple knowledge is powerful. It can move mountains. We can rejoice.

We can have gratitude in our hearts for all God's sustaining grace, for all God's goodness from day to day. We can look around and count our blessings, starting with the glass of water on the table next to us.

It really is impossible to be in a miserable mood when we start thanking God for little things.

We may be in great pain and even in agony, but deep down in our hearts, the joy keeps flowing. Joy is like a song that just keeps singing.

If you need this joy, it is yours for the asking because in the Gospels we read:

"Ask, and it shall be given to you; seek, and you shall find; knock and the door shall be opened to you, for everyone that asks, receives, and he that seeks finds, and he that knocks, the door is opened to." (Matthew 7:8)

So ask for the joy that you need, and you will receive it.

CHAPTER SEVEN

THIS ILLNESS:

Is it to Die Or For God's Glory?

"Whether we eat or drink, it is for the glory of God; in life and in death we are the Lord's." (1 Corinthians 10:31, Romans 14:8)

What kind of illness do you have, my friend?

Is it a terminal illness, such as cancer or AIDS?

Have you been definitively told by a doctor that you have six months to live, or do you have an ongoing "chronic" condition that has lasted for many years, such as fibromyalgia or multiple sclerosis? Either way, pain and illness are a part of your life.

Maybe you are not suffering from physical illness per se but from a mental affliction, such as depression, anxiety, or trauma. Regardless of your present pain or illness, just for a second, so that we can gain the right perspective, we can hearken back to the earlier pages of this book, to all that has been written about the purpose of this pain.

As we have said, all our sufferings and pains in loving and following Jesus are for eternal purposes. Through them, we can help to spread God's kingdom, just as we are, right in our circumstances.

But, if you have been given a diagnosis of terminal illness, such as cancer or AIDS, you would be on a different road and trajectory, as compared to someone who is slogging it out day to day with chronic fatigue syndrome or depression, right?

Here's what I want you to know:

If you have been given a terminal diagnosis, you are getting ready to meet God.

You could probably read many books about the dying process and how to prepare to die peacefully.

Many such books have been written about how to put your house in order, so to speak, like getting closure with all your "unfinished business." Clear up any unresolved or unreconciled issues with your kids, husband, or siblings, for example.

But this book isn't specifically about how to die well, though we can touch on that subject briefly.

First things first, my friend, whatever you are dealing with, whether it is a chronic or terminal illness or prolonged pain of any sort, just be where you are. Practice radical acceptance of exactly whatever is going on right now and of everything happening now. Remember that acceptance is an active word, a conscious, deliberate choice at this present moment. You may have to express your feelings of sadness, anger, or confusion in order to reach radical acceptance and peace, but expressing your feelings is truly okay and necessary. Find someone to talk to, like a good friend, chaplain, or counselor. They will be able to help you on your journey toward peace.

 Finding acceptance is a process. It may take some time, but as you slowly and gently work through your feelings honestly and in whatever ways you can, you will reach your goal of finding acceptance. When you feel great pain in your body or sickness in your soul, don't fight against it. Try to accept it. This may seem impossible at first, but do your best. You may want to write in a journal or find a way to express your feelings by doing some form of artwork. Just do what works and what will help you feel better.

In any given circumstance, remind yourself that God has a purpose.

Do your best to accept where you are and work with what is presented to you in your current situation.

Acceptance doesn't mean we must like or agree with what is happening. We just have to say "Yes," like the Blessed Mary Ever-Virgin did, to whatever is happening in our lives and to whatever we are experiencing at any given moment.

Do your best to align your will with God's will in the moments and days you have, and pray for peace in anything that confronts you.

God will not leave you alone in your pain. If you open your heart sincerely, God will help you. In any situation, in whatever road you are on, whether it be that you are getting ready to die or that you are coping with a chronic illness, radical acceptance will help you to have peace. Be open to grace in the moments and days you have, and God will meet you right where you are.

Jesus, Mary, and Saint Joseph, together with all the angels and Saints, are always here to help you, no matter what. They will never leave you alone in your pain. They will always stay close by your side.

CHAPTER EIGHT

STAYING THE COURSE ON YOUR HEALING JOURNEY

"Love never fails."

(1 Corinithians 13:8)

Ultimately, regardless of the type of illness you have, whether chronic or terminal, I think the journey is all about healing.

When we die, we go to meet God and be embraced in His everlasting love and goodness.

When we live out our days on earth, we are here to live to glorify God.

We are here on this earth, for as long as we are here, to learn to love God and one another.

Death, in a certain sense, is the ultimate healing since when we depart this life and leave our mortal bodies and our suffering minds behind, we will be free of this earthly pain. As it says in Revelations 21, there will be no pain, no tears, and no sorrows in the next life, and God is creating a new heaven and a new earth.

So, in my way of seeing it, the entire journey is all about healing. We are on a pilgrimage to God. Healing is what awaits us. In the loving arms of God when we finally meet God in heaven. Peace is what Jesus promised us. Peace was Jesus' final will and testament. "Peace I leave you; my peace I give you." (John 14:27)

We have inherited love and comfort as children of God. Love, peace, hope, and comfort are what God wants to give us, no matter where we are on our journey and no matter what we are experiencing at this moment. We must hold onto these gifts and lean on the Lord since He is always there, ready to help us.

On my healing journey, I have been given so many graces. In this little book, I have tried to share them with you.

All these wonderful blessings of hope, I truly pray and wish for you, my friend!

Stay the course, one step at a time with God.

Stay close to Jesus in the day and in the night.

Stay in the healing light of God.

www.ingramcontent.com/pod-product-compliance
Lightning Source LLC
Chambersburg PA
CBHW070357310726
48977CB00002B/479